THE AMUSEMENT PARK MYSTERY
created by
GERTRUDE CHANDLER WARNER

Illustrated by Charles Tang

Albert Whitman & Company
Morton Grove, Illinois

Library of Congress Cataloging-in-Publication Data

Warner, Gertrude Chandler, 1890-1979.
The amusement park mystery / created by
Gertrude Chandler Warner ; illustrated by
Charles Tang.
p. cm.
Summary: The Aldens search for carousel
horses that have disappeared from an
amusement park.
ISBN 0-8075-0320-7 (hardback). —
ISBN 0-8075-0319-3 (paperback).
[1. Amusement parks—Fiction. 2. Mystery
and detective stories.] I. Tang, Charles,
ill. II. Title.
PZ7.W244Am 1992
[Fic]—dc20   91-5161
                              CIP
                              AC

Cover art by David Cunningham.

Contents

CHAPTER 1

The Guest House

"Wake up, Benny," Henry said, gently shaking Benny's shoulder. "We're here."

Benny yawned and sat up. "Has the bus stopped?"

"Look outside," Violet said, leaning across the aisle and pointing at the trees. "See? The trees have stopped moving past the window." She swung her lavender sweater around her shoulders and stood up.

Jessie reached for her bag, which was under the seat, and slid across to the aisle. "I'm eager to see Joe and Alice Alden, aren't you?"

"Yes," Violet said. "It's been a long time since we've seen our cousins."

As they moved up the aisle to the front door, Henry said, "It was nice of them to invite us, wasn't it?"

"Yes," Jessie said. "We had such good times on Surprise Island."

"And camping out and finding Bill McGregor," Benny said, wide awake and looking out the window. "I can't wait to go to the amusement park that's near Joe and Alice's." Then he rubbed his nose. "I'm sorry, though, that we had to leave Watch with Grandfather."

"Watch will be fine, Benny," Henry said reassuringly. "Our dog will keep Grand-father company. And Mrs. McGregor will look after both of them."

Jessie patted Benny's hand. "One of the first places we'll visit will be the amusement park, Benny."

Benny's face brightened.

"Step lively!" the bus driver ordered.

They took the big step down off the bus and onto the ground.

"Where're Joe and Alice?" Violet asked, looking around.

"Oh, they'll be here," Jessie said. "They're always on time."

Henry glanced about the bus station and noticed a big sign with the town's name, Pine Grove. Suddenly he broke into a wide smile. "Right over there," he shouted, pointing at a handsome young man.

Benny waved wildly. "Hi, Joe!"

"Hi, Benny!" a young man called, rushing forward and swinging the six-year-old boy around in a circle. Benny yelled with delight.

"Hello, Joe," Henry said, stepping forward.

Joe grabbed Henry's hand. "It's good to see you, Henry." He stepped back and studied the boy. "You're almost as tall as me!"

Henry's dark eyes sparkled. "Well, I *am* fourteen."

Joe shook his head and turned to Jessie. He brushed the girl's cheek with a kiss. "What a young lady you've become, Jessie! It's hard to believe you're twelve years old and Violet is ten."

Jessie smiled. "I'm glad to see you, Joe. Where's Alice?"

"She's working at the museum, but she'll be home in time for dinner," Joe said.

The young man looked over Jessie's shoulder and drew Violet forward.

Violet's cheeks grew pink. "Hello, Joe," she said shyly.

"You can tell you and Jessie are sisters with that brown hair and those brown eyes."

"Just like you, Joe," Jessie said, a twinkle in her eye.

Joe laughed as he threw their suitcases in the back of his station wagon. "Welcome to Pine Grove," he said. "I'll show you around after you've unpacked and had a cold drink. Even in the North Woods it's hot in August."

The children scrambled into the large car, and Joe drove down Main Street. Pine Grove was a pretty town surrounded by large pine trees. The children were all eyes as they rode past the library, the drugstore, the grocery store, a dress shop, and the Indian Museum where both Joe and Alice worked.

They hadn't gone very far down the highway when Benny shouted, "Look! There's a man in trouble."

There on the side of the road was a pickup truck with its hood up. The back end was loaded with cameras, stands, and lights.

Joe braked the station wagon and got out. "Hi," he called. "Can I help?"

A tall man with a red cap poked his head around the hood. "No, thanks," he said with a smile. "I already called a tow truck, and it should be here any minute."

Benny had already jumped out and was studying the equipment on the truck. "Are you a picture-taker?" he asked.

The man threw back his head and laughed. "Me? Naw, I don't know a thing about photography, my boy. I'm just delivering the stuff."

"Oh," Benny said. "I see." Losing interest, he climbed back into the station wagon.

Joe returned to the driver's seat, and they started off. He made a right turn, then a left, and slowed down when he went by the Pine Grove Amusement Park.

"Oh, boy!" Benny exclaimed. "Can we go

to the park and eat cotton candy?"

"You bet," Joe said. "I thought you kids might enjoy biking there tomorrow."

"Biking?" Henry asked.

Joe chuckled. "Yes, Henry and Jessie can use our bikes and I've rented two more."

"Hurrah for Joe!" Benny said.

Soon he pulled up to a white house with a large front porch and a swing. Around the house and yard was a white picket fence.

"Here we are," Joe said. "Everyone out for a glass of apple cider!"

"Wonderful!" Jessie said. "I could drink a gallon!"

Violet smiled. "At least a glass, Jessie."

They went into the house.

"How cozy!" Violet exclaimed, looking at the dark blue flowered loveseat and matching sofa, and the striped blue, yellow, and green easy chairs.

"It is pretty, isn't it?" Jessie said.

"Let's go outside," Joe said. "And I'll show you where you'll be staying."

Henry glanced at Jessie not knowing what to expect, but when they went through the kitchen and out the back door, they were both surprised. There was a charming little house, the exact twin of Joe and Alice's house, only smaller.

"It's the guest house," Joe explained, "complete with a kitchen. Do you like it?"

"Do we!" Benny said. "It's great!"

"Oh, yes," Violet said. "We can do our own cooking!"

Joe said, "I know how you like to be on your own."

They explored the little house. The two bedrooms were each done in blue. The living room had a large comfortable sofa, and nearby were two easy chairs. In the kitchen there was an eating nook in a large bay window. There was a small refrigerator and stove and cupboards with glass doors that displayed turquoise and pink pottery dishes.

After the Aldens had unpacked and hung up their clothes, they came back to the main house and drank apple cider with Joe.

Benny held out his chipped cup for more. "I never go any place without my pink cup," he announced.

Joe smiled. "And why is that?"

"I found this cup in a junk heap when we were living in the boxcar," Benny answered.

Joe nodded solemnly, pouring the cold juice into Benny's cup. "I remember the story of the boxcar. Your grandfather told me that you lived there because you were afraid of him."

"Yes," Jessie said. "After we lost our parents, we thought it would be better to live alone, rather than live with Grandfather."

"We thought he was mean and wouldn't like us," Violet added.

Henry chuckled. "Nothing could have been further from the truth."

"It was lucky Grandfather found us," Benny chimed in.

"Yes," Joe agreed. "Your grandfather Alden is a fine man."

"Is he your grandfather, too?" Benny asked, a frown crossing his round face.

"No," Joe replied. "My father and your grandfather were brothers."

"So our grandfather is your uncle," Violet said thoughtfully.

"Yes." Joe nodded. "Your grandfather is my uncle James Alden."

The back door opened and footsteps were heard coming across the kitchen and dining room. "Here you are!" Alice exclaimed, coming into the room. "We were counting the days until you arrived. Welcome, Aldens!"

"Hi, dear," Joe said, offering her a glass. "Will you have some cider with us?"

"Sure will," Alice said, collapsing in a chair. She wore jeans and a cotton shirt. "I'm thirsty after working in that musty museum all day." She smiled at each of the children. "You all look marvelous," she said.

"So do you," Jessie said, admiring Alice's slim figure and the light brown hair that curled softly about her face.

Alice laughed, a silvery tinkly sound. "Are you hungry?" she asked, rising.

"Starved!" Benny said.

"Benny, hush," Violet said.

"But I *am* hungry," he replied. "Honest!"

"Good for you, Benny," Joe said. "We've planned a hearty dinner for you."

"May we help?" Henry asked.

"Why, yes," Alice said. "Thank you."

"First, though," Jessie asked, "may we call Grandfather and tell him we arrived safely?"

"Of course," Alice said, pointing to the phone on a table in the living room. "Help yourselves."

They each spoke to their grandfather, telling him they were happily settled in, and promising to call him later in the week.

Re-entering the kitchen, the Aldens were each given a task. Benny set the table, Henry poured milk and water, Violet folded napkins, and Jessie made the salad.

Then the children sat down to eat. They were pleased with the hot delicious dinner that Joe and Alice had prepared — steak, baked potatoes, spinach, tossed salad, and banana-cream pie.

After dinner Benny leaned back and rubbed his stomach. "I'm not hungry anymore," he said, his eyes half closing. "I'm sleepy."

Alice sipped her coffee. "Well, you'd better get a good night's sleep because tomorrow you'll have a busy day."

Benny's face looked puzzled. "We will?"

"Yes," Joe said. "You're going to the amusement park."

"Oh, that will be wonderful," Violet said, rising to help Alice clear the table.

"Wait until you see the beautiful merry-go-round horses," Alice said.

Benny's eyes widened. "Horses?"

"Yes," Joe said with a chuckle. "The wooden horses on the carousel are hand-carved."

Alice's eyes shone. "The horses are really a piece of Americana."

"Americana?" Violet asked.

"Yes," Alice said. "A piece of American history or American art. The horses are not only very old but also very valuable."

"Oh, I can't wait to see them," Violet said.

"I can't wait to *ride* them," Benny echoed.

"Tomorrow we'll not only *see* the horses but ride them as well," Jessie promised, smiling.

"Tomorrow should be fun," Henry said, putting a hand on Benny's shoulder.

CHAPTER 2

The Merry-go-round

On Tuesday morning, in their cabin, the Alden children prepared a big breakfast of orange juice, pancakes, maple syrup, sausage, and milk. Alice had stocked the refrigerator and cupboards with enough groceries to last two days.

"Are you ready to go to the amusement park, Benny?" Jessie asked.

"Yes!" he answered. "I want to eat cotton candy and ride on the tilt-a-whirl and the merry-go-round!"

Violet laughed. "Aren't you afraid you'll get dizzy?"

Benny grinned. "Nope! I could ride the tilt-a-whirl all day long!"

Jessie scraped her plate at the sink. She wore jeans and a white T-shirt. Her thick hair bounced up and down when she walked.

Henry stood up from the table and stacked the rest of the plates. "Isn't this a nice house?" he asked.

"It's like a doll house," Violet replied, glancing around.

After the dishes were washed, Henry opened the door. "Let's begin the day. Alice and Joe are at work already," he said cheerfully.

They wheeled the bikes out of the garage and mounted them.

As they biked along the road with the sun streaming through the pine trees, Henry whistled a tune with Jessie joining in. Benny puckered up his lips, but no whistle came out. The harder he tried, the more his cheeks puffed out, the redder his face became, and the more air he blew out.

Violet laughed. "Don't feel bad, Benny. I can't whistle either."

Arriving at the amusement park, they put their bikes in a bike rack and carefully padlocked them.

The park opened early on summer mornings. Rides were whirling and twirling around them, lights flashed, and customers on the rides shrieked with delight.

"Ooooh," Benny gasped, running toward a concession stand. "Cotton candy."

The others followed and gathered around the stand. Benny gazed at the pink frothy candy oozing out of the machine. He looked up at Henry. "Could I have some?" he begged.

Henry smiled and shook his head. "It's a little early. But you've been dreaming about cotton candy ever since we arrived." He turned to a woman with dark hair and asked pleasantly, "We'll all have one. How much?"

The woman pointed to the sign as her bracelets jingled. She wore her hair pulled tightly back into a bun, showing gold earrings. She handed each of them a cone of cotton candy.

"My, my," a man with black curly hair

said to Benny, "that cone is almost as big as you are." He winked at Henry and took the money. Smoothing down his drooping moustache, he questioned, "Where are you kids from?"

"We're staying just outside Pine Grove," Violet answered shyly.

"Yes," Jessie said in a friendly tone. "We're visiting our cousins."

"Welcome to Pine Grove," he said, holding out his hand to Henry. "I'm Frank Arnold and this is my wife, Sheila."

"I'm Benny Alden," Benny piped up.

Henry laughed. "And I'm Henry Alden, and these are my sisters, Violet and Jessie."

"We serve hamburgers and hot dogs, too," Sheila Arnold interrupted in a husky voice. "Come back for lunch."

"Oh, we will," Benny said happily, licking the giant pink cone of candy.

They walked over to the Ferris wheel. "That's the biggest Ferris wheel I've ever seen," Violet exclaimed.

Jessie, turning to her left said, "Oh, look, there's a House of Mirrors!"

A young woman with straight red hair who was standing there glanced at Jessie. "I knew people would love this!"

"Let's go in," Henry said.

"Sorry," the unsmiling woman said abruptly, turning away. "It's new and won't be open until tomorrow."

"Look!" Benny yelled. "The merry-go-round!"

The children hurried away, forgetting all about the unpleasant woman. They stared at the graceful carved horses.

"They're so lifelike," Violet breathed, completely won over by the horses' beauty.

The calliope music blared forth as the horses moved up and down to the musical beat.

"I've never *seen* such beautiful horses," Henry said in an awed tone.

"And to think," Violet added, "Alice said they are part of our history."

Jessie marveled at a large brown and gray steed. The gallant horse had plates of armor painted on and armor over his head so that only his eyes and ears were visible.

"I want to ride that gray one with the dots!" Benny said eagerly. "It looks like he's breathing fire."

"That's called a dapple gray, Benny," Jessie explained.

"It's hard to choose a favorite," Violet said, studying them. "They're all so beautiful."

They rode the merry-go-round twice, then dismounted and rode the swings and the Ferris wheel. The Ferris wheel frightened Benny a little. They ate hot dogs and chocolate shakes and trudged over every inch of the dusty grounds.

Several times they stopped to try their luck at different games. Henry threw a softball, knocked down five wooden milk bottles, and won a box of candy. Jessie put money in a machine full of prizes and maneuvered a huge claw to pick up a silver ring with a green stone. Violet tried her hand at the ringtoss and managed to circle three pegs, winning a small but cute teddy bear. Benny had his weight guessed, but the man guessed wrong, so Benny won a softball.

By midafternoon the children were tired.

"I'm ready to go home," Jessie said, brushing a wisp of hair from her forehead.

"Me, too," Benny said. "I was ready after that scary Ferris wheel ride."

Henry led the way to the bikes, and even though the Aldens were weary, they pedaled along the road, filled with contentment. It had been a wonderful day.

When Joe and Alice got home the Aldens told them every detail about the rides, the food, and their prizes. The day had been filled with surprises, but Joe had a surprise, too.

"We're having a barbecue tonight," he said.

"Yes," Alice said. "Joshua Eaton and his daughter, Karen, are joining us. They own the amusement park."

"Oh, great," Violet said, her eyes sparkling. "Maybe they'll tell us something about the merry-go-round horses."

"I hope so!" Jessie said. "Let's go to our house and clean up."

After Henry had given Joe and Alice the box of candy he'd won, the children left.

Once they'd washed and put on clean clothes, they came back to help with dinner.

Jessie was placing the silverware on the table when the doorbell rang.

A gray-haired man and a young woman of about twenty entered. Benny blurted out, "Why, you're the girl we saw by the House of Mirrors."

"Yes, I am," she replied with a flicker of a smile.

"Hello! Hello!" the gray-haired man said. "I'm Joshua Eaton."

"And these are our cousins," Alice said, presenting Violet, Jessie, Henry, and Benny.

The children said hello. "Wow," Benny said. "You own the amusement park! I won a softball!"

"Good for you," Joshua Eaton said.

"Please, everyone, sit down and make yourselves comfortable," Alice said. "Before dinner we'll have a glass of tomato juice."

"And," Joe said, bringing in a plate, "crackers and cheese."

Joshua Eaton leaned forward. "How did

you kids like my amusement park?"

"It was great," Jessie said, looking especially nice in a pink sweater and white shorts.

"The horses on the merry-go-round are beautiful," Violet said.

"Ah," Joshua said, settling into his chair. "I'm glad to hear you like my carousel. You know, those horses were carved by the Dentzel Company a long time ago, and are extremely valuable."

Karen gave a bitter little laugh. "Those horses!" she sneered. "Who cares about some dumb wooden horses! I keep telling Dad that we have to modernize. No one rides the merry-go-round except little kids, and it's mostly teenagers who come to the park."

Benny sat up straight and glared at Karen. "Little kids are important, too! And I loved the merry-go-round horses."

"And *I* loved the merry-go-round," Jessie said, a hint of defiance in her voice.

"An amusement park without a carousel wouldn't be much fun," Violet said.

"You see, dear," Joshua said mildly, facing

his daughter. "We must keep our valuable carousel."

Karen sniffed and tossed back her long red hair. Her green sweater brought out the freckles on her oval face. Jessie thought Karen's face could be pretty if she would smile once in a while.

"Well," Karen said stiffly, "we'll see which will get more use, the House of Mirrors or the merry-go-round."

Joshua sighed as if he and his daughter had had this argument many times.

"The horses are very different from the horses I've seen on other carousels," Henry said.

Joshua chuckled. "Yes, most horses are painted bright colors and trimmed with gold, but the Dentzel horses are usually gray or brown."

"Tell us about Mr. Dentzel," Jessie said.

Joshua smiled at the Aldens, pleased that they liked his horses as much as he did. He ran his fingers through his silver hair and began. "Gustav Dentzel was born in Germany. He came to America and settled in

Philadelphia. He and his brother, son, and nephews started the Dentzel Company in 1867."

"The horses are old!" Benny exclaimed.

"Very old," Joshua said, smiling at Benny. "In the Dentzel Company one man carved the bodies, another the legs, and Gustav's brother assembled the horses." He glanced at Henry. "Gustav's brother's name was Henry, too."

"How many Dentzel merry-go-rounds are there?" Alice asked.

"Very few are in operation today," Joshua answered. "The company only produced two carousels a year. The Dentzel horses," he continued, "have a distinctive style. They were carved in what is called 'The Philadelphia Style.' "

"The Dentzel animals are so lifelike," Violet said.

Benny nodded. "I thought the horse I rode today could breathe fire."

Joshua laughed. "It's true, Benny. Sometimes it looks like the horses could gallop right off the carousel."

"Is the company still in business?" Henry questioned.

Karen snorted disdainfully. "No, thank heaven, or we'd be buying *more* horses. After Gustav Dentzel died, his son, William 'Hobbyhorse' Dentzel took over. When he died in 1928, the company ended."

"How sad," Violet said thoughtfully. "I wish they'd kept on carving more beautiful horses."

"With the money we'd earn from selling the horses," Karen said, "we could install up-to-date rides. We could even add a roller coaster. Teenagers want more exciting rides than what we have." She frowned at her father. "You have to get with the times, Dad. Who cares about Dentzel's old horses?"

"I do!" Benny said in a very loud voice. "I *love* the horses." He looked pleadingly at Joshua. "Please, Mr. Eaton, don't *ever* sell them!"

Joshua reached over and squeezed Benny's knee. "As long as I'm around," he promised reassuringly, "the horses will be around, too!"

Jessie glanced at Karen's face. Joshua's daughter's green eyes flashed, and her mouth twisted downward. For a moment Jessie felt a twinge of sadness. Because of Karen's determination to update the park, Jessie wondered if Karen would be able to talk Joshua Eaton into selling his wonderful horses.

CHAPTER 3

The Deserted Barn

Wednesday morning, after a breakfast of waffles and milk, Jessie and Henry biked to the store for groceries. They walked through the aisles, pushing a cart and picking up bread, milk, hamburger, chicken, buns, lettuce, tomatoes, apples, lemons, chocolate chip cookies, eggs, orange juice, green beans, and corn on the cob. At the deli counter, they bought ham.

When they returned, bike baskets over-flowing with grocery bags, they saw Violet and Benny sitting in the porch swing of Joe and Alice's house. Benny jumped off the porch and dashed toward them.

"See what we've brought," Henry called, pedaling around the back.

"Hurrah for food!" Benny shouted, running around the house to the guest house. He danced around Henry, craning his neck to see what he had brought.

Violet ran after Jessie.

Pulling out one sack after another, Benny asked, "What are we going to do today?"

Violet, setting the gallon of milk in the refrigerator, turned and smiled at Benny. "What would you like to do?"

"Go on a picnic," Benny promptly replied.

"What a good idea," Violet said, placing the apples in a bowl.

"Yes!" Jessie said, tossing up a lemon and catching it, "and I'll make the lemonade."

"Look," Violet said. "Ham for sandwiches."

"And," Benny said, reaching for the cookies, "cookies for dessert."

Violet busily set to work making up four sandwiches, while Jessie squeezed lemons and added water and sugar to the juice.

Henry filled four small sacks each with a sandwich and an apple, and Benny added two cookies.

"Let's not go by the amusement park," Benny said, "or I'll want to stop."

"Then we'll head in the opposite direction," Henry said.

In his bike's basket Henry carried a big thermos, three paper cups, and his lunch bag. Benny carried his lunch bag and his pink cup. Jessie carried her lunch bag, a rolled-up tablecloth, and four napkins. Violet carried her lunch bag and paper plates.

As they pedaled, Jessie pointed to a dirt side road. "Let's go down that lane. It looks lovely with those elm trees lining both sides."

"Yes!" Benny shouted. "We'll explore new lands!"

They laughed and sang all the way down the narrow winding road. Overhanging branches shaded them. They pedaled by a meadow with grazing black and white cows. The yellow field appeared golden in the bright sunlight.

After they had been traveling for a few

miles, Benny suddenly groaned. "I'm starving. Are we ever going to stop?"

"Yes, Benny," Violet answered. "I'm ready to stop, too."

Henry veered left. "Over there," he shouted. "There's a brook and a grove of trees."

"Perfect!" Jessie said, biking ahead and leaning her bike against a tree.

She lifted out the tablecloth, which she spread on the soft green grass. Violet set out plates while Henry poured the lemonade. Benny put a sandwich on each plate.

Sitting cross-legged, Benny smiled with contentment. "This is nice," he said. "I can hear the little creek rushing over the rocks."

"Yes, this is a perfect spot," Jessie said, gazing over the green grass and the blue water beyond. In the distance was a red barn trimmed in white.

"I wish I had brought my paints," Violet said.

The tree branches swayed gently in the warm breeze, and nearby a meadowlark trilled a sweet song.

After eating, Henry stretched out while Jessie and Benny ran to the little brook. The water was so clear that they could see the pebbles and sand on the bottom. Before Violet could join them, the little boy and his big sister had slipped off their sneakers and socks, rolled up their jeans, and waded into the water.

"Ohhh, it's c-cold," Benny stammered.

"Soon it will feel okay," Jessie reassured him.

It wasn't long before Violet splashed into the water, also. Wading downstream, they found smooth pretty pebbles.

At last they came ashore and lay on the bank. In a few minutes, Jessie propped herself up on her elbows. "I wonder what's in that barn," she said lazily.

"Let's find out!" Benny said with excitement.

"Right!" Violet said, turning to look for Henry. "Henry! Come here."

"I heard you," he said, standing behind her and chuckling. "I'm ready to check out the red barn. It looks deserted." He motioned to Benny, and the two boys dashed ahead.

Once in the quiet barn, the children gazed at the sunbeams dancing with dust particles. The clean barn floor appeared to be unused. The stalls were brand-new, and fresh hay was piled inside. No one was around. Not a horse. Not a cow. Not even the farmer. There were no tools. The barn was empty.

"Where is everyone?" Benny whispered.

Henry poked his head around one of the stalls and said, "I don't know, Benny."

The smell of fresh hay filled the air as they explored the empty barn.

Finally, Jessie said, "Let's leave. This place gives me the creeps." They quickly left, puzzled by the silence and the emptiness.

Once they had biked home, they saw Joe and Alice, watering and weeding the flowers in front of the house.

"Hi, kids, come on in for a cold glass of juice," Alice called, wiping her forehead. She wore gardener's gloves and held a watering can.

"Gladly!" Benny shouted, dismounting

his bike and running toward the house.

The others quickly followed.

Sitting around the table, the Aldens drank the juice and relaxed.

Jessie said, "Today we saw an unusual place."

Alice, her brown eyes smiling, looked at her. "What kind of a place?"

"A big red barn!" Benny blurted out.

"Yes," Henry said. "We picnicked near a stream west of here."

"And we explored a nearby barn," Violet finished. "It had fresh hay, but it was completely empty!"

"Ah," Joe said, leaning back. "I know the place. The barn belongs to Old Jim Mitchell, an eccentric man, who lives alone. He doesn't have any cows or horses and I've often wondered why he has such a big barn."

"What could Old Jim be up to?" Alice wondered.

"It's a mystery!" Benny said, a big smile crossing his face. "I love mysteries!"

Jessie smiled. "Benny, maybe there's no mystery at all. Maybe this Old Jim just likes to have a barn for storing things."

Violet glanced at Jessie. Perhaps her sister was right. And yet remembering the way the deserted barn looked sent a shiver up her spine.

CHAPTER 4

Peter McKenzie

The next morning the Alden children biked to Clear Lake, which was a small lake in Pine Grove Park.

Arriving at the park with the lake shimmering before them, they eagerly jumped off their bikes. They hurriedly stripped down to the swimsuits they wore underneath their clothes.

As they ran toward the blue-green water, they heard voices. A man and woman were sitting on the sandy bank. The young man said, "But each horse is worth a fortune!"

The girl replied, "Yes, but you know how

my father feels about the merry-go-round."

The young man said, "I like the dapple gray, don't you?"

The girl emphatically said, "*No!* Not the dapple gray, the brown, or any other color." She sighed. "If it were up to me I'd get rid of the carousel. We could sell those horses and make a lot of money. But my father . . ." Her words quickly trailed off as she glanced backward and spied the Aldens.

Jessie stopped in her tracks. "Why, Karen, it's you!" She wondered if Karen would do anything against her father's wishes.

"Hello," Karen said smoothly, rising to her feet and tossing back her red hair. "Please, come and meet my friend Peter McKenzie."

"Hi, kids," the young man said, a lopsided smile spreading across his handsome face. He had long black hair and wore khaki pants, sneakers, and a white short-sleeved shirt.

"Meet Henry, Jessie, Violet, and Benny," Karen said, introducing each of them. "What are you doing here?"

"We're going swimming at the lake," Violet answered with a smile.

"Want to go in the lake with us?" Benny questioned, his sturdy legs planted far apart. His red trunks looked even redder against the yellow towel slung over his shoulders.

Peter turned and stared at Benny. A grin broke across his tanned face. "Not today, partner. I've got to go back to work."

"Do you work near here?" Jessie asked.

"Sure do," he responded. "I'm a golf pro at the Old Oaks Country Club."

"Do you teach golf?" Henry asked, tossing the beach ball he'd brought up in the air and catching it. "I'd like to learn to play golf someday myself."

Peter raised heavy brows over his dark eyes. "If you want a lesson, look me up."

"We will," Henry said. "That would be great."

"I'd like to learn, too," Jessie added.

"I've got the time," he said cheerfully. "Today I only teach one lesson. I'm not earning much money, as you can see."

"Let's go, Peter," Karen said, taking his arm. "I want to check the House of Mirrors."

"Karen, you have the most fun job of all," Benny said.

Karen looked at Benny. "I like my job, but," she added with annoyance, "I'd like it better if the amusement park showed a bigger profit." With these words she and Peter hurried away.

Jessie watched as Karen and Peter disappeared among the trees. She didn't like the sound of Karen's words. Was money the only thing Karen was interested in?

"Come on in the water, Jessie!" Benny yelled.

"Be right there," Jessie answered. And forgetting Peter and Karen, she laughingly raced into the water and splashed Benny.

The children played together for quite a while, then Jessie and Violet swam out to a raft that was anchored down by ropes. They jumped up on the raft and lay on their backs with their faces to the sun.

Henry and Benny played catch with the beach ball. The morning flew by. When it was time to get out of the water, Benny held back. "Can't we stay in longer?" he begged.

Henry shook his head. "Violet and Jessie are coming in. It's almost time for lunch. Later we're going to the amusement park. Don't you want to go?"

"Oh, yes," Benny said, wrinkling his sunburned nose. "I forgot." He waded as fast as he could to the bank.

It was such a warm and sunny day that they took their time pedaling home.

Once in the house they all helped with lunch. Jessie broiled hot dogs, Violet toasted the buns, Henry poured the milk, and Benny set out the mustard, relish, and ketchup. Dessert was cherry pie.

After lunch, Benny leaned back. "Ummmm," he said, rubbing his stomach. "That tasted good."

"Are you sleepy, Benny?" Violet asked.

"A little," Benny murmured.

"We'd better forget about the amusement park," Jessie teased.

"No! No!" Benny shouted, his eyes opening wide. "I want to ride the merry-go-round on that pretty dotted gray horse." He glanced at Jessie. "I mean the dapple gray one."

Jessie laughed. "You remembered, Benny. Yes, you can ride the dapple gray. Twice if you want to."

So about two o'clock the children again mounted their bikes and headed for the park. From the distance they could hear the calliope music, and they began to pedal faster.

When they arrived, Benny ran to the cotton candy stand.

"Well," Sheila Arnold said, "if it isn't the Aldens again."

"A cotton candy, please," Benny ordered.

Sheila filled a cone with pink frothy sugar.

Frank chuckled. "Glad you like our stand, my boy. Come back as often as you like."

"I like the merry-go-round best of all . . . better even than cotton candy," Benny said.

Sheila glanced at Frank and said quickly, "I need some help here, Frank. Stop gabbing!"

Frank nodded, and didn't say another word. Violet wondered why Sheila was grouchy all of a sudden. Maybe she just didn't like little kids. Some people didn't.

After Benny had his candy, he and Jessie went over to the tilt-a-whirl with Violet and

Henry trailing behind. It wasn't long before the four of them were seated in a round tilt-a-whirl car with Benny in the middle. Soon the ride started. At first, the car made a slow half turn, then it picked up speed and whirled one way, twirled another, and spun all the way around. Benny screamed with delight. Henry and Violet laughed so hard their sides hurt. When the car came to a halt, Jessie wiped her eyes. "Oh, that was fun," she gasped, trying to catch her breath.

As soon as they walked down the ramp, Benny dashed toward the merry-go-round to watch the beautiful horses go up and down and round and round.

When the merry-go-round stopped, Jessie and Violet walked toward it. All at once Jessie noticed Peter McKenzie studying the painted horses. She pointed at the young man who was holding a sketch pad.

Violet said, "Oh, let's say hello."

"Yes, let's," Jessie agreed, quickening her step.

Peter was so intent in sketching the horses that he didn't see them at first.

Violet, always interested in art, was eager to see what Peter had drawn.

As the two girls moved closer to Peter, he glanced up. Hastily he slammed shut his sketch book and jumped to his feet. "Hello, Jessie and Violet," he said, taking a step backward. "I-I'm late," he added quickly, and turned on his heel.

Strange, Jessie thought. Why didn't Peter want us to see his drawing of the horses? And why was he sketching them anyway? Something mysterious was in the air. The music started again. Now the drumbeat kept time not only to the rise and fall of the horses, but also to the rapid beating of her heart.

CHAPTER 5

Mystery at the Merry-go-round

Violet and Jessie stared after Peter as he hurried away.

"Will you go on the merry-go-round with me?" Benny asked, jumping up and down.

"Yes," Violet answered, "but I think Jessie and I will sit in the swan chariot." She needed to talk to Jessie about Peter Mc-Kenzie's strange behavior.

"That's okay," Benny said with a smile.

So Benny rode the dapple gray, while Henry rode the chocolate brown charger. Henry's fancy horse had a silky mane with a small carved angel clinging to the saddle.

"Wheee, here we go!" Benny shouted,

slapping the horse's side as if he could make it go faster.

Once underway, Benny held on to the mane, and every once in a while he reached down and touched the jewels tacked onto the bridle. Laughing at the horse's up and down motion, Benny lifted his head high.

Sitting in the chariot, Violet asked, "Why do you suppose Peter wouldn't let us see his sketch? He acted as if it were a secret."

Jessie looked puzzled. "I know. I don't know what he was trying to hide. It's only a carousel horse."

After the ride, the children walked over to the House of Mirrors. Henry bought four tickets, and they entered Karen's latest improvement to the amusement park.

When they reached the first mirror, Benny gazed at himself. His eyes widened and his mouth formed a big O as he saw his funny image. There he stood, a tall thin figure, wavering back and forth.

Jessie, Violet, and Henry, three skinny tall forms, slipped by Benny and went into the corridors of hundreds of mirrors.

Wandering off alone, Violet stopped before a mirror. Her hand flew to her mouth at the sight of herself. The slender young girl was changed into a short squat person with a head that looked like a squashed pumpkin.

Giggling, Violet pointed at herself, unable to believe what she saw. "Henry!" she called.

Her brother hurried around a group of mirrors and stared at Violet's image. He laughed. "Violet, is that you?"

She nodded, then laughing, pointed to his reflection. The tall boy was now short and fat. He looked as if he were three feet tall and three feet wide. Henry grinned. "We make a weird pair!"

"Jessie," Henry said, raising his voice. "Come, look."

But Jessie wasn't in sight.

Violet, Henry, and Benny all turned a corner to see where Jessie had gone, but when they wended their way down one path, they were faced with more mirrors. They tried another way, but it was the same. Mirrors in front, mirrors in back, mirrors to the right, and mirrors to the left.

"Jessie!" Henry shouted, glancing around. No answer.

"Jessie!" Benny yelled. "Where are you?" He fearfully glanced at Henry. "She's gone."

"I'm here," came the faint response.

They weaved around one mirror, only to be faced with another.

Henry bit his underlip. "Where could she be?" he murmured.

"Jessie!" Violet said, her voice trembling, her heart pounding. She was beginning to feel frightened.

This time Jessie's voice was loud and clear. "Here I am," she said, stepping out from behind several mirrors.

"Jessie," Benny shouted, running to her. "We thought you were lost." He smiled at her. "I was scared."

Jessie nodded. "I was beginning to think so myself."

From then on the four of them stuck together. After a few false starts they finally discovered their way to the exit.

Outside, Violet said to Benny, "Are you ready to go home?"

"Not yet," he said. "Could I ride one more time on the merry-go-round?"

"Sure, you can," Henry said. "We'll watch from here."

"Did you pick out a horse you like?" Jessie asked.

Benny nodded and pointed to a light colored horse with a lovely red and turquoise saddle blanket. "I'll give the dapple gray a rest. I want to ride the white one this time."

Violet smiled. "It looks white, doesn't it? But it's really a very pale gray."

Henry bought Benny a ticket, and the small boy ran to his chosen steed. Quickly he placed a foot in the stirrup and swung a small leg over the saddle.

The music began and the horses bobbed up and down. But as Henry, Jessie, and Violet watched, they were surprised to see that Benny's horse stayed in one place. The gray horse went around in a circle with the others, but it didn't move up and down.

Benny, digging his heels into the horse's flanks, tried to make it move. Finally, he stopped and looked down at his horse. With a puzzled frown he glanced around. All the other horses were going up and down. Disappointed, he simply sat and waited for the ride to be over.

When the merry-go-round halted, Benny slid off his horse and came running. "The dumb horse didn't move!" he complained.

Jessie studied the horse. None of the horses had ever been motionless before. Every one had moved up and down. What was wrong with this horse?

She glanced at Violet, who was chewing her underlip. Evidently Violet, too, thought something was wrong.

"I think we should tell Joshua," Violet said.

For a moment Jessie didn't speak, then she said thoughtfully, "Maybe it just needs oiling," she said. "Joshua probably knows and the horse will be fixed tomorrow."

"Okay, Jessie," Henry said. He was puzzled, however, as he gazed at the horse. He hoped Jessie was right, and that it was just a little problem.

CHAPTER 6

Who Hurt Benny's Horse?

Several days passed before the Aldens returned to the amusement park. The first place they stopped was at the concession stand.

"Oh," Sheila said, "are you children back again?"

"Yes!" Benny said promptly, hopping up on the stool. "We haven't been here for two whole days." He grinned. "I missed my cotton candy." Then his smile faded. "The last time I was here one of the horses wouldn't work!"

"What do you mean?" Sheila asked.

"The horse Benny rode wouldn't go up and down," Violet explained.

"Oh," Sheila said, frowning. She turned her back, clearly not wanting to talk anymore.

"Ah," Frank said, coming in from the back. "If it isn't Benny Alden." He scooped lots of cotton candy in a cone. "This is for you!" He held out the gigantic pink frothy cone.

"Oh, my," Violet said. "Look at that, Benny! Can you eat it all?"

"Just watch me!" Benny said, eagerly reaching for the cone. "Ummmm, it's good," he said, licking contentedly.

Jessie laughed. "Come along, Benny."

Henry said, "Listen to the calliope music."

Benny smiled, pink foam ringing his mouth. "The merry-go-round! Let's go for a ride," he said gleefully.

They walked down the dusty pathway with rides and games on either side of them.

"Don't you want to try a different ride?" Jessie asked, heading for the swings.

Benny lapped up the rest of his cone and

turned in the direction of the swings. "I don't know," he said doubtfully.

"We rode them when we first came," Violet reminded him, "and you thought it was fun."

"Okay," Benny said, agreeably.

Henry bought four tickets, lifted Benny up into a swing, and strapped him in. Then he, Jessie, and Violet found swings behind Benny and the ride began.

The swings, attached by chains to a center pole, flew out a little from the ground. Then as the swings picked up speed, they flew faster and faster and higher and higher above the ground.

Violet laughed. "Everything's a blur."

The swings spun at a dizzy rate.

Gradually the swings whirled slower and slower as they came to a halt.

Henry jumped down and helped Benny out.

Benny staggered a bit, and his face was white. "That was scary!" He held his head.

"But it's fun to go so fast, isn't it, Benny?" Violet asked.

"No," Benny said in a firm voice. "I like the merry-go-round better. The horses gallop at just the right speed."

"Then the merry-go-round it will be," Jessie said. "You can pick out any horse you like."

Benny's face lit up. "I want the dapple gray again. He's my favorite."

So again they all rode horses and enjoyed the bobbing movement and the loud calliope music.

When they dismounted, however, Violet was surprised to see Benny looking unhappy. Bending down, she asked, "What's wrong, Benny? Your horse went up and down this time, didn't it?"

"Yes," Benny replied seriously, his lower lip trembling, "but someone cut my horse's side."

"What?" Henry exclaimed, jumping on the platform to examine Benny's horse.

Henry ran his hand over the horse's side. There was a long scratch that reached from the horse's head to the saddle.

"Hey!" an unshaven man yelled. "If you

want to go on the merry-go-round, buy a ticket! Look what happens when I take a couple of days off. Nobody watches what's going on!"

Henry gave the cross man a smile and jumped off.

"You're right, Benny. The dapple gray has a deep scratch on its side." Henry studied Benny's face. "Are you sure that mark wasn't there before?"

"I'm sure!" Benny said. "I know every inch of my horse!"

The children were quiet as they walked out of the park. Then Henry said, "I'm sorry about your horse, Benny. Who could have done such a thing?"

"I wish we knew," Violet said. "It's too bad."

When they were on their bikes, Jessie asked, "Do you think it could have been scratched on purpose?" When she saw Benny's sad face, she quickly changed the subject. "You know, we have a chicken to make for dinner tonight. Why don't we invite — ?"

"Joe and Alice?" Violet finished, her eyes sparkling.

"Right you are," Jessie said.

"Great idea," Henry said.

"Oh, boy, company," Benny said and he smiled, forgetting about his scratched horse.

Benny begged to be the one to visit the main house and ask Joe and Alice for dinner.

Jessie said, "Of course, you may!"

When they reached their house, the children set to work to make an extra-special dinner.

Alice had given them permission to pick flowers from her garden, so Violet promised to pick a bouquet of carnations and roses for the centerpiece.

"Good," Jessie said. She had hoped that Violet would volunteer as she always arranged things so well.

By six o'clock, the chicken was roasting in the oven, almost done. Henry and Benny had set the table and arranged the chairs.

When Joe and Alice came in, Alice smiled. "Oh, how lovely," she said. "This is a perfect ending to a busy day."

"Why were you so busy?" Benny asked, looking clean and handsome in his navy blue jogging suit.

Joe sat down at the table and said, "We had a school group tour the museum today." He paused. "But you must have been busy, too. What have you been up to?"

Jessie laughed. "Fun things, like the amusement park."

"I don't think Sheila Arnold likes us," Benny said suddenly.

"Why do you think that?" Joe asked.

"I don't know," Benny said. Then after a thoughtful pause he added, "But she frowns a lot."

"Maybe she just had a bad day," Joe answered with a smile.

Violet passed the chicken to Alice. "This looks positively delicious," Alice said. "You even put flowers on the table and lit candles. I can't believe you did all this!"

"It was fun," Henry said.

"Yes," Jessie said. "And we always work a little harder when we know we're having company."

The dinner turned out well. The chicken was juicy, the salad crisp, the peas not overcooked, and the mashed potatoes smooth and creamy.

For dessert Jessie and Henry served ice cream with chocolate sauce.

"What rides did you go on today, Benny?" Joe asked, taking a spoonful of ice cream.

Benny wrinkled his nose. "The swings. I don't like the swings anymore! I felt like I was falling out. I like the merry-go-round best."

Alice asked, "Do you have a favorite horse?"

"Oh, yes," Benny said. "The dapple gray."

"Ah," Joe said, pushing back his empty ice cream dish and sitting back. "You even know the horse's color."

"I do," Benny answered. "Today, though, the dapple gray had a big scratch on its side." He shook his head sadly. "I was upset."

Concerned, Alice glanced at Benny. "I don't blame you. A scratch on a beautiful horse! I wonder how it got there."

"Probably some careless rider," said Joe. "You really enjoy the merry-go-round, don't you? I know you hate to see any of the horses hurt."

"Yes," Violet answered. "They're too beautiful."

"When Gustav Dentzel first introduced his merry-go-round, did everyone find it as magnificent?" Jessie asked.

"Yes, indeed." Joe stopped and chuckled. "Well, almost."

"Almost?" Henry said. "You mean someone *didn't* like it?"

"It seems Gustav Dentzel was so proud of his spectacular horses that he took them on a tour," Joe said. "Once, when he traveled to Richmond, Virginia, the calliope started to play, and little boys, instead of riding his merry-go-round, threw stones at it."

"Threw stones!" Benny echoed, wide-eyed.

"Yes," Joe continued. "You see, Dentzel's music played 'Marching Through Georgia.' This was a Yankee war song about General Sherman's burning of Atlanta."

"That song was a no-no in the South," Alice said.

"Believe me, Dentzel learned his lesson and never played music that would offend anyone," Joe said with a laugh.

"Well, I hope his carousel and calliope music go on forever," Violet said, smiling.

"So do I," Henry said. But secretly he was worried. Already one horse didn't go up and down, and another had been scratched. Was someone hurting these beautiful horses?

CHAPTER 7

The Unpainted Horse

Early in the morning Henry said, "You know, I think Joshua needs to know about the scratch on the dapple gray and the horse that doesn't go up and down."

"You're right," Jessie said.

"If we go now, the park won't be too busy, will it?" Violet asked.

"We'll have to find Joshua right away," Henry said. "He'll be around."

"Good!" Benny said. He sneezed twice.

"You'd better wear a sweater and take a handkerchief," Violet said.

Benny, without an argument, slipped on

his sweater and tucked a handkerchief in his pants' pocket. "I've never seen the park with the rides quiet," he said.

"Today's the day," Henry said lightly.

So after a hearty breakfast of orange juice, oatmeal, and toast, the children biked to the park.

When they entered, the rides were motionless. Only a few people were around. As they passed the concession stand, Sheila was busy cleaning the cotton candy machine.

"Good morning," the Aldens called pleasantly.

"Morning," Sheila muttered, scarcely looking up.

Benny whispered, "I told you she didn't like us."

They walked toward the merry-go-round where Ned, the man who ran it, sat perched on the platform, munching on a doughnut. He wore a black vest over a shirt with the sleeves rolled up. He looked up, surprised to see anyone in the park. "We're not open," he said gruffly, taking another bite.

"We need to see Joshua," Violet said politely. "Could you tell us where he is?"

Ned jerked a thumb over his shoulder. "He's back in the trailer."

"Thank you," Jessie said.

The man grunted and took a gulp of coffee.

Benny raced ahead and knocked on the trailer door.

Joshua opened the door and said, "Well, if it isn't the Aldens. Come in."

The cozy trailer had a bedroom and a stainless steel kitchen with a table in the corner and a cushioned bench around it.

"Have a seat," Joshua urged, smiling at them. "This is an unexpected pleasure."

"We have bad news for you," Benny said, his mouth turned downward.

Joshua's eyebrows shot up. "Bad news?"

"Yes," Jessie said. "Benny has discovered two things about your horses that aren't right."

"And what is that?" Joshua said, sitting down and folding his hands.

Benny answered, "One of your horses doesn't go up and down."

Joshua frowned. "Is that so? I hadn't noticed. I've been too busy working on the House of Mirrors."

Benny cleared his throat.

"And what else?" Joshua asked.

"The dapple gray has a big scratch on its side," Benny said.

"My word!" Joshua said, with a worried tone. "You're very observant, Benny."

"Yes, he is," Violet said. "We thought you should know that something is wrong with your valuable horses."

"I'm glad you told me," Joshua said, standing up. "Let's take a look."

They filed out of the small trailer door and hurried to the merry-go-round.

"Ned," Joshua said, "start her up, will you?"

With a sigh, Ned crushed his paper sack between two big hands, and tossed it in the trash can. He went to the switch and flipped it on. The merry-go-round started.

Joshua observed the pale gray horse. "Ned," he said worriedly, "that horse isn't moving."

Ned shrugged. "So what's the big deal?"

Joshua frowned, jumped up on the carousel, and examined the dapple gray. "Turn it off, Ned," Joshua said grimly, his eyes darkening. "This is bad. Two of my Dentzel horses have been damaged."

"What do you mean?" Ned grumbled. "Just because a horse doesn't go up and down doesn't mean it's damaged. Some kids like a horse that stands still."

"Not me!" Benny exclaimed.

Ned glared at him.

"And that scratch," Joshua said after he examined the horse. "I don't understand how a scratch that long could happen accidentally."

Benny's eyes grew big. "You mean someone hurt your horses on purpose?"

"Maybe," Joshua said, his lips tightening. "One horse doesn't go up and down, and suddenly there's a scratch on another one. It's strange, I have to admit."

"Who knows how long that scratch has been there?" Ned snapped. "I think you're all crazy."

"No," Joshua said calmly. "That scratch

is brand-new. I know it. I intend to find out how it happened."

"Yes, the scratch is new," Benny said firmly. "*I* know that scratch wasn't there before, 'cause I've been riding the dapple gray all the time." He looked up at Joshua. "We'll help you find who did this!"

Joshua managed a smile. "Thanks, Benny. That would be wonderful if you would help me."

"We will," Benny said.

"I appreciate how you came all the way over here to tell me," Joshua said. "I believe you're more concerned than my daughter."

"I'll bet if Karen knew about it, she'd be upset, too!" Benny said.

"I doubt it," Joshua said miserably. "She's more interested in the House of Mirrors." He shook his head. "And now she's talking to me about putting in a small roller coaster."

"A roller coaster!" Violet said with astonishment. "That would take a lot of space!"

"It would take up half the park," Henry said in dismay.

"I know," Joshua said grimly. "But right

now, all I can think about is my horses."

"I'm sure it will work out," Jessie said reassuringly.

Joshua gave her a weak smile, but he looked doubtful.

Henry sat on the edge of the merry-go-round platform, ignoring Ned who was tinkering with the machinery.

I wish I could help Joshua, Benny thought. He looks so sad, and he's such a nice man. He pulled his handkerchief from his pocket, but just as he was about to sneeze a breeze came up, whisking the white square out of his hand.

The handkerchief flew through the air and landed on the floor of the merry-go-round. Without a second's wait, Benny yelled, "My handkerchief!" and rushed forward, hopping up on the platform. The linen square, however, escaped from his fingers and fluttered beneath the chocolate brown horse. Benny crawled on all fours after it.

He reached for the handkerchief, grasping it. "I got it!" he shouted triumphantly. Then he happened to look up at the horse's un-

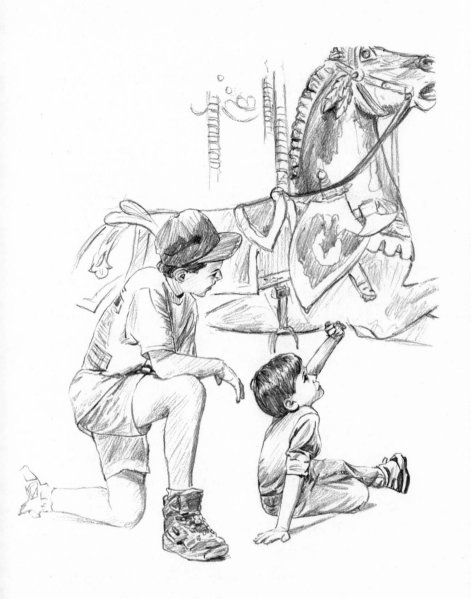

derside. Benny scrambled backwards and said in an excited voice, "The horse's stomach doesn't have any paint on it! It's all bare wood."

Henry glanced at Benny in astonishment. Then he quickly dashed forward. Ducking his head, he examined the horse. "Benny's right," he called out.

Standing up, Henry said in a puzzled tone, "That beautiful horse isn't finished. Someone left it only partly painted."

"Surely Gustav Dentzel would carefully paint every inch of his horses," Jessie said, a frown crossing her face.

"Oh, no," Joshua Eaton groaned, checking out the horse for himself.

Violet's heart felt heavy. Had another horse of Joshua's been tampered with? Who would do such a thing to this splendid carousel?

Just then Ned joined them. "What's the matter now?" he asked in an annoyed tone.

"The brown horse isn't completely painted," Henry said. He didn't like talking to Ned. The man was short-tempered and didn't seem to care at all about the merry-go-round he operated.

"This is terrible," Joshua said. "Dentzel would never have sold an imperfect horse."

"What are you so upset about?" Ned growled with a shrug. "It's only a couple of merry-go-round horses."

But it was plain that Joshua *was* upset.

"We'd better go home," Jessie urged.

Joshua nodded absentmindedly as he walked away with his head down.

Leaving the amusement park, the children glimpsed Karen, carrying a clipboard. She was checking the House of Mirrors entrance. She glanced up but seemed to look right past the Aldens as she hurried on.

Jessie gave a discouraged sigh. If Karen had her way, a roller coaster would be installed. Then the amusement park wouldn't be the same.

CHAPTER 8

A Frightening Phone Call

After their trip to the amusement park, the children biked home.

After opening the door, Benny ran in and threw himself on the sofa. "I feel bad," he said.

"Do you have a cold?" Henry asked.

"No." Benny's voice was muffled as he pulled the pillow over his head. "I feel bad for Joshua and his horses."

"I know," Henry said soothingly. "It's a shame we can't find out who's hurting the horses."

Just then the phone rang.

"I'll get it," Jessie said, jumping up from her chair.

"Hello," she answered.

For a moment she only listened. Then she said angrily, "Who *is* this?"

Benny sat up. Henry looked at Jessie inquiringly. Violet hurried in from the kitchen, halting when she saw Jessie talking on the phone.

Suddenly Jessie slammed down the telephone.

Wide-eyed, Benny asked, "Who was it?"

Quietly, Jessie sat down, stunned. Then she spoke. "It was this awful deep voice warning us to keep away from the amusement park."

"*What?*" Henry said.

Jessie's face was white as she repeated the caller's words. "He said, 'Don't come back to the amusement park.' "

"The nerve!" Violet said, her dark eyes blazing with anger.

Benny leapt to his feet, his hands on his hips. "This is a free country! We'll go to the amusement park *anytime* we want to."

"Right, Benny!" Jessie said, her chin jutting out with determination.

"We won't be scared off!" Violet said firmly.

"Who do you suppose doesn't want us near the park?" Henry asked. "And why?"

The children spent the afternoon playing Monopoly, but their minds were on the phone call. Every once in a while Jessie glanced anxiously at the phone as if afraid it would ring again.

Just after Violet won the game, someone knocked on the door.

Benny rushed to answer. He flung open the door. His eyes were wide. "Hi, Joe," he said. "Hi, Alice."

"Come in," Violet said.

"Oh, we're so happy to see you," Jessie said. Then she told them about the terrible phone call, her words tumbling over one another.

"And," Benny added, "today we saw a merry-go-round horse whose stomach wasn't painted."

Joe's eyebrows rose. "What's happening at

the old amusement park?" he questioned with a worried frown darkening his face.

"Maybe you *should* stay away from the park for a while," Alice said nervously. "I don't like the sound of what's going on over there."

"I agree," Joe said soberly. "We have to think about this." Seeing the worried look on the children's faces, he added, "But we've got to eat. Let's go to Mike's Spaghetti House for supper, go to a movie, and on the way home we'll stop for ice cream."

"Oh, boy," Benny said, clapping his hands. "Could we?"

"Of course, we can," Joe said.

Violet laughed. "That's a wonderful idea. We'll forget all about phone calls and carousel horses."

"I'd love to spend an evening like that," Jessie said gratefully.

Alice managed a smile. "You're right, Joe. We need to forget about the park tonight."

"Then it's settled," Joe said. "Mike makes the best spaghetti sauce in town, and at the Pine Grove theater there's a new movie called, *The Robot Who Had a Heart*."

"Perfect," Henry said with a grin.

"We'll leave in thirty minutes," Alice said. "Will you be ready?"

"I'll be ready in five," Benny said quickly.

Jessie laughed. "Thirty minutes will be fine."

And in half an hour the children had washed and dressed. Violet's lavender ribbons in her hair matched her T-shirt. Jessie wore a green top and jeans. Her long hair was pulled back with a green ribbon. Henry, all in white from his T-shirt to his sneakers, had on a red sweatshirt. And Benny, in red jeans and a blue-and-white T-shirt, looked very patriotic.

"I'm ready!" Benny said.

And so were Violet, Jessie, and Henry.

Their dinner at Mike's was just as good as Joe had promised, and the movie had lots of exciting scenes. Afterward they stopped at an ice-cream parlor and ate scrumptious butterscotch sundaes, piled high with whipped cream and nuts.

On the way home Jessie sank into the backseat of the station wagon and said, "What a wonderful evening. I didn't think of that awful phone call one time!" She smiled contentedly. "Thank you, Joe and Alice."

"Yes, thanks," Benny echoed. "Wasn't it exciting when the robot caught the mean guy and twirled him around?"

"Yes," Alice said, her eyes twinkling. "I'm glad we went. Joe and I have been working hard at the museum, too, and a night out did us all good." She glanced at her watch. "Do you know it's past midnight?"

As they drove past the dark amusement park, closed for the night, Joe suddenly slowed down. "Look," he said, pointing in the direction of the park.

Flashes of light brightened a corner of the park. "How weird," Violet said. "What is it?"

The bright light continued to go on and off.

"I don't know," Benny said. "Maybe it's a spaceship."

Alice laughed. "I don't think so, Benny. But I can't figure it out either."

"Could it be a flash camera?" Henry asked.

"Why would someone be taking pictures at night?" Jessie asked in a puzzled voice.

"You know, Henry, I think you're right," Joe said. "The light seems like the light from a flash camera."

"I still don't know why anyone would be taking pictures this late," Jessie said.

Joe nodded. "It is odd! I wonder why," he said.

"Maybe," Henry said thoughtfully, "this person doesn't want to be noticed taking pictures in daylight."

"I don't like it," Joe said.

"Remember when we first got here?" Jessie said. "We saw that truck that had broken down. It had lots of camera equipment in it."

"Right," Violet said. "And that man said he was delivering the equipment to someone."

"But to who?" Benny asked.

Joe interrupted. "Wait a minute. That truck may have had nothing to do with what we're seeing now."

"Maybe we should tell Joshua," Jessie said.

The flashes of light stopped and all was quiet.

"Not tonight," Joe said. "Let him get a good night's sleep. Anyway, whoever's in the park will just disappear if we go in."

"We'll go to the park first thing tomorrow and tell Joshua," Jessie promised.

When they returned home, the children went directly to their little guest house. The strange lights were still on everyone's mind.

"I wish we knew what was going on," Henry said, dropping into a chair.

"Do you think it has something to do with the horses?" Benny asked in a trembling voice. "I don't want anything to happen to my beautiful horses."

"None of us do," Jessie said, agreeing with Benny. She sat cross-legged in front of the chair. "But look at all the strange things that have happened around the merry-go-round."

"Even Sheila," Violet said, "seemed upset when she heard one of the horses wouldn't go up and down."

"And now it turns out *three* of the horses

are damaged," Henry said, frowning in thought.

"And someone's sneaking in the park at night to take pictures and to hurt the horses," Benny said, his chin in his hands. "This is getting weirder and weirder."

"Yes, it is," Violet said.

"So weird," Jessie said, "that I think we'd better go to bed and sleep on it."

"I won't sleep!" Benny announced.

Henry stood up and stretched. "Oh, I think you will, Benny. Come on, let's get in our pajamas."

"And we'll go to the park tomorrow," Jessie promised. "Joshua might be able to shed some light on what's going on."

Maybe, Violet thought. But she doubted it. Joshua seemed as confused as they were.

CHAPTER 9

The Expert

After their late night out the children slept later than usual the next morning.

Henry mixed up a batch of pancakes, Violet broiled the sausages, Jessie poured the orange juice, and Benny set the table.

After they had eaten, they rode their bicycles to the amusement park to tell Joshua about what they'd seen.

Henry pedaled faster to pull alongside Jessie. "Shall we tell Joshua about your phone call?"

Jessie shook her head. "You know, I feel

sorry for Joshua. He has enough to worry about. Let's keep the phone call our little secret."

"I think you're right," Henry said.

When they arrived, they parked their bicycles and walked by the concession stand. Sheila spotted them right away. "Are you back again?" she said in disbelief. "You'd think this place was your second home."

Jessie glanced at her but didn't answer. She kept walking. So did Benny, Violet, and Henry. Sheila certainly didn't welcome them to the park. "Isn't it funny," she asked, "that Sheila is so unfriendly?"

"It is," Henry said.

"Do you think she could be the one who phoned us?" Violet asked.

"It was a man's voice," Jessie answered.

"I wonder if we'll ever find out who it was," Violet said.

"I'm sure we will." Jessie's response was positive.

At last they spotted Joshua. His gray hair ruffled by the breeze, he stood chatting with Ned by the merry-go-round.

"Hi, Aldens," he called. "Before we open the park, do you want a free ride?"

Violet smiled. "Thanks, but not today, Mr. Eaton. We need to talk to you."

Joshua gave them a quick look. "Okay, come over and have a seat." He sat down on the merry-go-round's platform.

Ned pushed back his hat and stared at them for a few seconds. Then without a word he walked away to the coffee stand.

Benny sat down next to Joshua, but his brother and sisters stood. "Well," Joshua said, glancing at their faces. "What's wrong?"

"Last night," Henry said, "when we drove by the closed park, we — "

"We saw," Benny interrupted, "the sky lit up with lights."

Joshua frowned. "What was it?"

"We think someone might have been taking flash pictures," Jessie explained.

Joshua looked confused. "What is going on?" he said. "I think I need to do something about this!"

Karen, wearing white jeans and a green short-sleeved sweater, stepped out of the

House of Mirrors and joined them. "Hi,
Dad." She glanced at the children. "Hello,
Aldens," she said without smiling.

"Hello," Jessie said, shifting uneasily from
one foot to the other. She wasn't comfortable
around Karen. She knew how Karen felt
about the merry-go-round and wasn't sure if
she'd care about her father getting to the bottom of this.

"Karen," Joshua said calmly, "the children
told me that someone took flash pictures here
last night. Something is definitely going on.
Three of my horses have been tampered
with!"

Karen raised her eyebrows. "Three?"

Boldly, Benny spoke up. "Yes, three! The
light gray doesn't go up and down. The dapple gray has a big scratch, and the chocolate
brown's stomach isn't painted!"

"Is that so?" Karen replied, hands on her
hips and head tilted to one side. A frown
crossed her freckled face and her red hair
shone crimson-gold in the sunlight. "It
doesn't sound too serious to me. It's probably
all coincidence."

"It *is* serious!" Benny exclaimed. "The horses are being hurt!"

Sighing, Karen glanced at her father. "Then I suppose you'll be checking into this."

"Those are valuable horses, Karen," Joshua retorted. His round cheerful face was changed into a scowl. "And I intend to find out something *today!*"

"You're not going to call the police, are you?" Karen asked, with concern. "That wouldn't be good for the park at all."

Joshua shook his head. "First I need to be sure. Last night I couldn't sleep worrying about this whole thing," Joshua said. "First thing this morning I carefully examined *all* the horses . . . the damaged ones and the perfect ones. I know those horses as well as I know my own name. Now I'm wondering if maybe the damaged horses aren't Dentzel's horses — if they might not be fakes. They don't look like Dentzel horses to me."

"*Fakes!*" Karen exclaimed. "I doubt that."

Joshua spoke rapidly. "One of the horses doesn't work properly, another is badly scratched, and the third is only partly painted." Joshua paused to catch his breath. "You can be sure the original horses were not like that."

"Oh, no!" Benny burst out.

Joshua was silent and then said, "I know what I have to do. There are experts in this field, people who would know if these are the real Dentzel horses or not. I have to find someone to examine my horses."

"Oh, Dad!" Karen said. "Of course these are the real horses. How could they not be? You paid enough for them."

"I don't know," Joshua said. "But I'm going to find out."

"Good!" Benny cried.

"I'll make some calls this afternoon," said Joshua. "Right now, I need to check on a new part we ordered for the Ferris wheel."

The next day, the Aldens went for a long bike ride along the Old Orchard Bike Trail.

Finally, Benny's legs grew tired. "I'm hungry," he complained.

"I'm tired, too," Violet said, slowing down.

They wheeled about and headed for home.

Once in the house Jessie dropped in a chair. "I'm too tired to eat lunch," she said.

"Not me!" Benny said. "I could eat two sandwiches."

Jessie laughed. When the phone rang, however, she became serious.

"I'll answer it," Henry said quickly, striding into the room and picking up the phone.

He listened to a deep voice growl at him, "This is a warning! Stop meddling at the amusement park!"

"Who is this?" Henry shouted. But the phone clicked and the line went dead. For a moment Henry stared angrily at the phone. Then he glanced at Jessie. "That must have been the same caller you had, Jessie. He had a deep voice and warned us to stay away from the park."

Numbly, Jessie nodded. "Oh, Henry, who could it be? These calls scare me."

Henry smiled grimly. "Don't worry, Jessie. We'll find the one doing the phoning."

"I hope so," Jessie said in a low voice. Inside, though, she wasn't sure that they'd ever know who was doing these awful things.

After lunch Violet said, "Let's go back to the park and see what's happening."

Benny asked, "You mean you're not afraid of mean Sheila or the phone calls?"

"I don't know if it's Sheila," Jessie said thoughtfully. "What about Ned? He never seems too happy to see us."

"It might be Karen," Violet said. "She doesn't care two cents for the merry-go-round. I think she'd do anything to get the money to put in the new roller coaster that she wants for the park. And why was Peter sketching the horses?"

"Let's go anyway," Henry said. "I want to see if Joshua found an expert to examine the horses."

"I doubt if he could locate a person with such special knowledge this soon," Jessie said. But she stood up.

"I'm ready," Benny said, one hand on the doorknob.

Bicycling to the park, they went right to

the carousel. Rides were whirling, and music was blaring on all sides.

Violet was the first to see the tall woman at the merry-go-round. Without a word, she pointed to her.

The big-boned woman was running her hands over the dapple gray. She peered at the horse's head and examined the body.

"Hi, Aldens," Joshua said, smiling. "This is Ms. Margaret Macy, an expert on Dentzel horses. I made lots of calls last night. Frank told me about this expert who happened to be staying at the Sunnyside Motel over at Watertown. She was on her way to Boston but I persuaded her to make a detour and come to Pine Grove. Wasn't I lucky to find someone on such short notice?"

Margaret Macy glanced at the children and smiled. Then she went back to her work. She didn't even pause long enough to say hello. Nodding, she methodically checked the horse's legs, ears, mouth, and eyes.

Violet thought it was quite a coincidence that Margaret Macy happened to be so near Pine Grove.

They all watched as Ms. Macy examined the three horses that had been damaged. She was very careful and finally she said to Joshua, "You don't have to worry, Mr. Eaton. These horses are *definitely* Dentzels. The scratch must have been made by someone who cleans the carousel. As far as the unpainted belly of one horse . . . well, Mr. Dentzel was human. He could make mistakes, too. The horse that doesn't go up and down has a mechanical problem, but he is a Dentzel horse."

Joshua Eaton smiled broadly and shook Ms. Macy's hand. "I can't thank you enough. You've made me very happy."

The Aldens were almost as happy as Joshua. Jessie and Violet hugged him, and Benny said, "I'm glad Ms. Macy was near here and could come right away."

CHAPTER 10

The Terrible Ferris Wheel Ride

When the children arrived home, Henry pulled an envelope out of the mailbox. "Hmmm," he said, bewildered, "this is funny. It's addressed: *'To the Aldens.'* "

"We got a letter," Benny cheered. "May I open it?"

"Sure," Henry said, handing it over.

Benny tore it open. His mouth formed a big O when he noticed the words had been cut out of newspapers.

Jessie, who was standing behind him, read the letter aloud.

"Aldens! Go home! You're snoopy and don't belong here! Don't return to the amusement park.

Signed,
THE WATCHER."

Jessie looked up. "How do you like that!" Benny gave the letter to Henry.

"This is unbelievable!" Violet said indignantly. "Shall we call the police?"

"Well," Henry said. "Maybe we should tell Joe and Alice."

"But nothing's happened to us," Jessie said. "And if we tell them, they might send us home."

Henry nodded. "We don't want to go home now, that's for sure." He paused. "Besides, I think we can solve this mystery ourselves."

"We'll keep our eyes open," Jessie said firmly. "And we'll find out what's going on."

"*We'll* become 'The Watchers,'" Benny said, pressing his lips together in a stubborn line.

Henry's smile was grim. "Yes, Benny. We

won't let a few phone calls and one letter keep us from going to the park."

A rap on the door interrupted them.

Hastily, Henry slipped the letter into his pocket as Jessie opened the door.

Alice stood before them. "I'm driving into town to buy a pair of sneakers," she said. "How would you like to ride along?"

"That would be fun!" Benny exclaimed.

"And maybe while you're waiting for me you'd like to order a chocolate ice cream soda at Lou's Drugstore." Alice's green eyes sparkled. "My treat."

"Yes!" Violet said with a smile.

"Yes," Jessie said with a wider smile.

"Yes," Henry said with a grin.

So the Aldens drove off with Alice, and as she shopped, they settled themselves at a round table in the window at Lou's. Soon they were served huge chocolate sodas.

While they ate, Violet suddenly put down her spoon. "Look," she said, finding it difficult to swallow, "there are Sheila and Frank."

Benny craned his neck. "Where?"

"At that table over there," Jessie said, her voice rising in surprise.

"They're with Margaret Macy!" Henry said.

Sure enough, the tall woman was seriously talking to Sheila and Frank.

"That's right," Henry said. "Frank is the one who told Joshua that Margaret Macy was in Watertown."

"Oh," Violet said. "Sheila's handing Ms. Macy an envelope."

"I wonder what's in it," Jessie said with a puzzled frown.

"I wonder, too," Benny said, drawing up on his straw for the last bit of chocolate ice cream soda. "Maybe they're handing Margaret Macy a card wishing her a good trip."

"I don't believe that," Jessie said. "Look, she's taking money out of the envelope and counting it!"

Sure enough the tall woman carefully counted the bills and, smiling, she stuffed them in her handbag.

"Do you think Joshua asked Frank to pay

her for inspecting the carousel?" Violet said.

"Why would he do that?" Jessie asked. "Why wouldn't Joshua just pay her himself? That doesn't make sense."

Henry tapped his chin with the straw. "I think Frank is paying Margaret Macy off."

"For doing what?" Benny questioned innocently.

"Maybe for pretending to be an expert, examining Joshua's horses, and saying they were real," Henry said.

"Why would Frank and Sheila do such a thing?" Violet asked.

"I don't know, but we'll find out," Henry said, his jaw set and determined.

The children watched Sheila, Frank, and Margaret Macy. They didn't talk long. Sheila kept glancing over her shoulder. Suddenly, her eyes rested on the Aldens. She said something to Frank and Ms. Macy, and the three of them left quickly.

"So, Margaret Macy was paid off to say the Dentzel horses were real." Violet shook her head in disbelief.

"And to think Joshua trusted her!" Jessie

straightened her shoulders indignantly. "Margaret Macy isn't an expert, after all! She's a crook!"

"He trusted Frank, too," Henry said. "He believed him when he said Ms. Macy was an expert."

"We'd better tell Alice!" Benny shouted.

Henry glanced at Benny, shaking his head. "We'd better not. She might not let us go back to the park and find Joshua. He should be the first to know and decide what to do."

Benny put his finger to his lips. "Not a word," he whispered.

So when Alice picked them up, the children raved about the sodas, but didn't mention a thing about what they'd seen.

When the Aldens arrived home, they mounted their bikes and pedaled to the park.

Sheila and Frank were at the concession stand, just as if nothing had happened. When Sheila spotted them, her dark eyes shot sparks in their direction.

"Frank and Sheila are watching us," Henry said, his lips barely moving. "Act natural."

"Shall I buy a cotton candy?" Benny asked.

"That's being very natural," Jessie said, chuckling. "Go ahead, Benny."

"Let's not find Joshua right away," Violet cautioned. "We don't want Frank and Sheila watching us."

"You're right, Violet," Jessie said. "We'll just go on a ride or something."

Benny joined them, happily licking his cotton candy. "Sheila was grumpy, but she took my money."

The children strolled down the dusty midway, the calliope music playing a brisk march. And all the while Violet's heart thumped.

"The carousel horses look beautiful in the sun," Jessie said, linking her arm through Violet's.

"Don't they?" Violet said in a shaky voice. "The chocolate brown shines like mahogany."

"Can I ride one of the fake horses?" Benny asked.

"Shhh," Henry said, "not so loud. I don't

think you'd better." He glanced at Sheila, who was watching them through narrowed eyes. "I think we'll stay away from the merry-go-round," Henry said thoughtfully.

"Pretend we're here to enjoy the park," Violet said. "We should act casual, so they won't suspect us."

"Why don't we ride the Ferris wheel?" Jessie asked.

Benny peered up through the spokes to the top of the Ferris wheel. "It's too tall," he complained.

"Yes," Henry answered. "And because it's so tall we'll be able to see the whole park." Then he leaned down next to Benny's ear and whispered, "We'll be able to keep an eye on Frank and Sheila."

"Okay," Benny agreed. "We can't be good detectives if we can't see what's going on."

Soon they were seated on the Ferris wheel, going up, up in the air.

At the top their chair gently rocked back and forth.

When they descended, it halted to let off

passengers. Once more they moved swiftly
around in a circle.

High on top of the Ferris wheel, the rides
and people looked small.

Violet glanced over the side and noticed
Sheila talking to the man who ran the ride.
After a few minutes, the man walked toward
the coffee stand. Sheila now ran the Ferris
wheel. Fearfully, Violet glanced at Jessie and
Henry, who nodded in understanding. They
had seen the man leave and Sheila take over,
too.

Again they climbed higher and higher. At
the top the Ferris wheel shuddered to a stop.

"I'm afraid to look down when we're at the
top," Benny confessed. He hugged Jessie
tight.

"I like to see everything!" Jessie said. "I
can see Sheila below!" She put her arm reassuringly around Benny.

Their chair swayed back and forth.

"All the other passengers have gotten off,"
Violet said, biting her underlip. "We're the
only ones on the Ferris wheel!"

"I know," Jessie replied, her pulse racing.

"I don't like this ride," Benny said.

Henry placed his hand over Benny's.

Sheila gazed up at them, her face twisted in a terrible smile.

Benny dared to peek over the side. "Sheila's going to keep us up here forever and ever," he whimpered in a frightened voice.

Henry tried to think of something he could do to make Sheila start the Ferris wheel again, but he couldn't. Benny started to cry, but he tried very hard not to sob too loud. Tears filled Violet's eyes, too, as she gazed at the ground that seemed so far away.

CHAPTER 11

Frank Tells All

Benny said between sobs, "Will we ever get down?"

"Sure we will," Henry said reassuringly. But when he looked down at Sheila's face, he had his doubts.

"Let us down!" Jessie shouted.

Frank Arnold dashed toward the wheel and grabbed his wife's arm. Sheila tried to shove him away, but Frank was too strong. For a moment the two struggled, then Frank grabbed the lever.

By this time a crowd had gathered and an alarmed Joshua rushed forward. In dismay he looked up at the frightened children.

Frank pushed the lever forward and the ride started. Down, down, the Ferris wheel came.

Violet sighed with relief and Jessie sank back against the seat. Their awful ride was over.

When they reached the bottom, the children scrambled out.

Stiffly, Benny straightened up. "My legs are wobbly," he said in a shaky voice. "I don't like the Ferris wheel!"

"It will be a long time before I ride it, too," Violet said.

"Thank heavens, you're safe," Joshua exclaimed, patting Benny's back. Then he turned to the Arnolds. "And you, Sheila!" he said angrily. "What did you think you were doing?"

Furious, she pressed her lips together and turned her back on him. Joshua faced Frank.

"Frank," Joshua said, "what's going on?"

Frank nervously smoothed down his moustache. "The carousel horses," he muttered. "They were the cause of everything!"

Joshua stared at him. "Go on," he said sternly.

"Frank!" Sheila shouted.

"We stole three of the Dentzel horses," Frank admitted, lowering his eyes. "I went along with the plan for the money. But when I saw the children at the top of the Ferris wheel, I changed my mind." He glanced shamefaced at Benny. "When it comes to hurting little kids, I draw the line!"

Sheila whirled around. "Frank! Be quiet!" she hissed. She shook her head fiercely, and the red scarf around her neck fluttered.

Frank gave her a sad look and murmured, "It's over, Sheila."

Joshua nodded firmly. "You bet it's over! We've known about the three damaged horses for some time." He shot the children a grateful glance. "Thanks to the Aldens. But we didn't know *you* were guilty. Where are my original horses?" Joshua asked in a forbidding tone.

"Frank!" Sheila screamed. "Not another word!"

Joshua half turned to Ned, who stood behind him. "Ned," he asked, "will you call the police?"

Ned shot Frank and Sheila Arnold a dark look, and said, "With pleasure."

Joshua turned back to Frank. "I'm waiting for you to answer my question. Where are my horses?"

"In Old Jim Mitchell's barn," Frank answered, then continued as if he wanted to get the whole story off his chest. "We had clever artists copy the real horses from the pictures we shot at night. When the carvers finished, they painted the fake horses just like the originals."

"Except," Benny piped up, "they forgot to paint one horse's stomach!"

Miserably Frank nodded. "You kids noticed every mistake that was made." He paused, then went on, "Everything was done at night. When the fake horses were ready, we substituted them for the original Dentzels." He sighed. "We were going to be rich!"

"If it hadn't been for these kids we would

have been!" Sheila glared at Benny. "You were always around the merry-go-round, no matter what I did!"

"Take it easy, Sheila," Frank said. "After the fake horses were in place on the carousel, we hired a truck to haul the original horses to the barn."

"Our biggest mistake was when we paid Margaret Macy in broad daylight. You kids even saw that!" He sighed. "Everything we did went wrong!"

Panic-stricken, Sheila dashed away.

"Stop!" Joshua yelled.

But Sheila kept running until she reached the House of Mirrors. She hurried inside.

"She's getting away!" Benny said, racing after her.

The other children followed. Joshua asked several bystanders to guard Frank, and hastily ran after the children.

Henry entered the House of Mirrors. "Benny," he shouted. "Where are you?" Benny, however, had already disappeared in the twists and turns and passages of the hundreds of mirrors.

Jessie and Violet stayed together, but Henry went after Benny.

Benny, on the trail of Sheila, tiptoed forward. As he came around a corner, he found himself face to face with a short fat boy. "It's me!" he squealed, and ran on, trying to find Sheila.

Hearing a noise, Benny whirled around, but no one was there. His stomach tightened in a knot. He was alone. "J-Jessie," he stammered.

No answer.

"Violet?" he called, raising his voice.

No answer.

"Henry!" he called in a louder tone.

No answer.

All at once Sheila appeared. Her eyes were wild and her red scarf was half untied and flapped around her face. "You!" she gasped, glaring at Benny.

Benny couldn't move.

Sheila grimaced and then vanished behind a mirror.

"Henry!" Benny yelled at the top of his lungs.

"I'm here!" Henry said, stepping from behind a mirror.

Benny turned around and saw a tall skinny Henry. He reached out, but his small hand touched cold glass. "Henry?"

"Here I am," Henry said, tapping Benny on the shoulder.

Benny sighed with relief. "Sheila was here!" he gasped.

"We'll stick together," Henry said. "Joshua's here, too."

And sure enough, Joshua seemed to step out of a mirror.

"Where did Sheila go?" Joshua asked urgently.

Benny shook his head. "She went in back of a mirror and just disappeared."

"We'll find her," Joshua said, his jaw square and set.

A slight rustling noise startled them. Henry turned one way, Benny another, and Joshua still another. "Who's there?" Benny cried.

"Come out!" Henry said in a forbidding voice.

Surprised, Violet and Jessie appeared before them.

"We're all together," Jessie exclaimed. "Didn't you see Sheila?"

"I did," Benny said proudly, "but she got away."

The five of them stood in the center of the House of Mirrors, wondering which way to turn.

All at once Violet put a finger to her lips. She nodded in Joshua's direction.

Slowly, Henry turned and glimpsed the tip of a red scarf.

"I see Sheila," Benny whispered.

"Stay close to me," Joshua said. "I know every passageway."

Jessie glanced at him. Did they dare approach Sheila? There was no telling what she might do.

CHAPTER 12

The Horses Come Back

Silently, Joshua moved toward the mirror where Sheila was hiding. The only movement was the quiver of the red scarf.

Suddenly Joshua flew around the corner and pounced on the woman. Henry followed. Sheila and Joshua scuffled, but Henry grabbed her arm and she stopped struggling.

"All right," she growled, yanking her arm free of Henry's grip. Henry recognized the suddenly gruff voice.

"I can tell *you* made the phone calls!" he said. "What a coward you are!"

"You kids were always interfering," she sneered. "I had to do something to stop you!" She glared at Henry. "But nothing kept you away from the amusement park. Not even my letter!"

"This way, Sheila!" Joshua ordered.

Henry, Jessie, and Violet walked on one side of Sheila while Joshua was on the other. Benny trailed behind.

"Just in case Sheila tries to escape," he said fiercely.

After Joshua explained to the waiting police what the Arnolds had done, they led Sheila and Frank away.

"Whew!" Benny said. "I'm glad that's over!"

All at once Karen raced across the grounds, flying into her father's arms. "Oh, Dad, I'm sorry I wanted to get rid of the merry-go-round. Ned told me about the thieves." She paused, gazing fondly at him. "I didn't realize how important it was to you."

"You'll keep the merry-go-round?" Benny asked, his brown eyes growing big.

Karen tossed back her red hair, laughing. "Yes, Benny. The carousel will be the main attraction in our park." She glanced at her father, her green eyes sparkling. "A roller coaster would take up too much space! I'll never complain about the horses again."

Joshua squeezed his daughter's hand. "You don't know how much this means to me, dear. The real horses are hidden in Old Jim's barn."

Karen's eyes glistened. "Let's go and get them."

"First, I'll need a truck," Joshua said, grinning.

"I'll call Peter. He'll rent one," Karen said. "Can't we all go out to the barn? If it hadn't been for the Aldens we wouldn't have discovered the three fake horses."

"Yes, indeed. The children are invited!" Joshua beamed at each of the Aldens. "This is the happiest day of my life," he said.

Within an hour, Peter drove up in a truck and the children piled in back. Joshua and Karen sat up front with Peter.

When they arrived at Old Jim's barn, they

couldn't see a sign of the horses.

"Where could they be?" Joshua asked with a puzzled frown.

Benny noticed a patch of gray shining through the straw piled in one of the stalls. He ran over and tossed straw in the air. "The dapple gray!" he exclaimed. "Here!"

Karen and Peter hurried into the next stall and brushed away the straw on the chocolate brown while Henry, Jessie, and Violet uncovered the pale gray.

Carefully, Joshua and Peter placed the dapple gray, the pale gray, and the chocolate brown horse on the truck.

Driving back to the amusement park, everyone felt happy and relieved. The mystery was solved. And the horses were safe.

Ned met them at the merry-go-round, and he and Joshua installed the precious Dentzel horses in their rightful places.

"Aren't they beautiful?" Violet said in a hushed tone.

"The most beautiful sight in the world," Jessie answered, standing back to admire the entire spectacular carousel.

Peter, standing with the Aldens, said, "Which is your favorite, Benny?"

"The dapple gray," he answered without a moment's hesitation.

"It so happens I have something for you," Peter said, his dark handsome face lighting up with a grin.

Benny tilted his head. "For me?" he asked, pleased.

"For you," Peter replied, taking a drawing from his sketchbook. With a big smile he held it out to Benny.

Benny's mouth dropped open in amazement. "Look," he said. "This is my dapple gray! It's beautiful!"

The others crowded around Benny. "Oh," Violet exclaimed. "What lovely lines. How real it looks!" Being interested in art, she could appreciate Peter's skill. She looked up at Peter. "Was this what you were drawing at the carousel that day?"

Peter grinned. "I like to draw. I wanted to surprise Benny with a sketch."

"We'll have it framed, Peter," Jessie promised. "And, Benny, won't it look beautiful

framed, and hanging above your bed?"

Benny, still gazing at his wonderful horse, said, "Yes! I'd like that!"

Happily, the Aldens returned to Joe and Alice's house. It was time to return to Grandfather's.

They related what had happened and Alice said, "We're proud of you. The Dentzel horses are part of our American history, and you've helped save them."

"We'll miss you," Joe said, reaching over and roughing up Benny's hair. "We didn't have a dull moment since your arrival!"

"We'll miss you, too," Jessie said, "but we'll come back again."

"You'd better," Alice said, chuckling.

That night the children packed, and the next day Joe drove them to the bus.

On the way back to Greenfield, each Alden had satisfied and happy thoughts. But all of them were glad that they had helped Joshua find his beautiful horses!

Benny couldn't wait to tell Grandfather the whole story. And to hug Watch!

GERTRUDE CHANDLER WARNER discovered when she was teaching that many readers who like an exciting story could find no books that were both easy and fun to read. She decided to try to meet this need, and her first book, *The Boxcar Children*, quickly proved she had succeeded.

Miss Warner drew on her own experiences to write each mystery. As a child she spent hours watching trains go by on the tracks opposite her family home. She often dreamed about what it would be like to set up housekeeping in a caboose or freight car — the situation the Alden children find themselves in.

When Miss Warner received requests for more adventures involving Henry, Jessie, Violet, and Benny Alden, she began additional stories. In each, she chose a special setting and introduced unusual or eccentric characters who liked the unpredictable.

While the mystery element is central to each of Miss Warner's books, she never thought of them as strictly juvenile mysteries. She liked to stress the Aldens' independence and resourcefulness and their solid New England devotion to using up and making do. The Aldens go about most of their adventures with as little adult supervision as possible — something else that delights young readers.

Miss Warner lived in Putnam, Connecticut, until her death in 1979. During her lifetime, she received hundreds of letters from girls and boys telling her how much they liked her books.